Ookie-Spooky

by Mirra Ginsburg

Based on a story by Korney Chukovsky

illustrated by Emily McCully

Crown Publishers, Inc.
New York

10 9 8 7 6 5 4 3 2 1

The text was adapted from the Russian <u>Biaka-Zakaliaka</u> by Korney Chukovsky.

The text of this book was set in Avant Garde Book and hand lettered. The four-color illustrations were prepared as line drawings with separations done by the artist for red, yellow, blue, and black halftone.

Library of Congress Cataloging in Publication Data

Ginsburg, Mirra.   Ookie-Spooky.   Summary: Masha draws many familiar things in her new drawing book but also something quite unusual. (1. Stories in rhyme) I. Chukovsky, Korney Ivanovich, 1882-1969. Zakaliaka. II. McCully, Emily Arnold.   III. Title.   PZ8.3.G4240o   (E)   79-14060   ISBN 0-517-53610-2

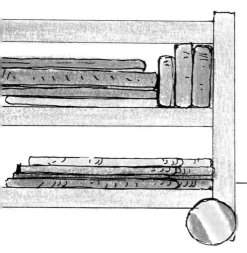

To Lydia Chukovskaya
and to Lyusha, Vera, and Mashenka
—M.G.

To Tad McCully, for his drawings
—E.M.

Mother gave Masha
a drawing book.
Masha started drawing.

This is a
woolly sheep

And this is baby
asleep

This is a house

And this is a mouse

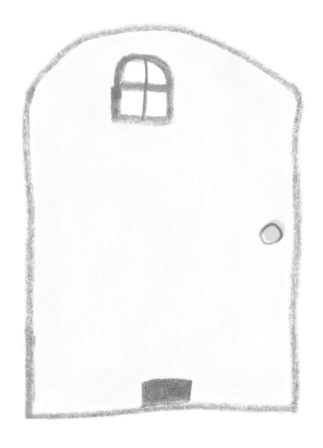

This is a door

And this is a store

This is mommy
and daddy

And this is
my dog Laddie

This is an
apple tree

And this is me!

And what is that?

It has whiskers...

but it's not a cat.

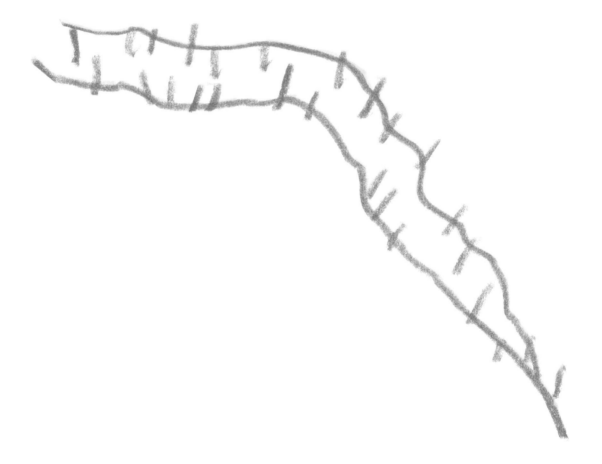

It has a tail...

but it's not a rat.

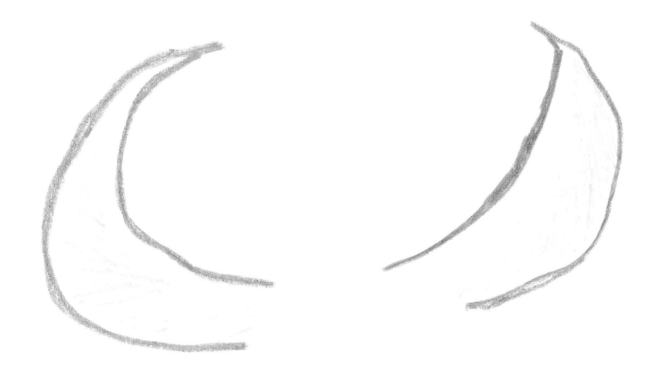

It has horns...

but it's not a bull.

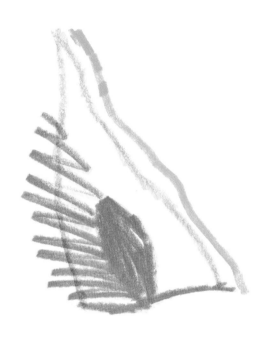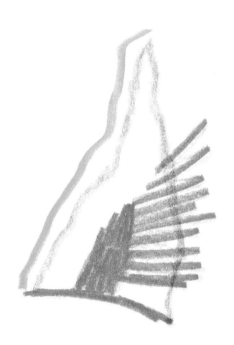

It has long ears...

but it's not a mule.

It has big teeth.

It has six feet.

Its face is red.

It looks like nothing living or dead.

It is Ookie
He is spooky
I made him up
Out of my head.

And why are you hiding
behind the bed?
Why did you throw
away the book?

I'm afraid

# of Ook!